DICK CLAIR

PREJUDICE

PUBLISH
AMERICA

PublishAmerica
Baltimore

First printing

ISBN: 1-4137-2707-7
PUBLISHED BY PUBLISHAMERICA, LLLP
www.publishamerica.com
Baltimore

Printed in the United States of America

DEDICATION

To Patrolman William Waterson, who's love of God, country and fellow man was ended all to soon in the line of duty.
May God bless you and all who serve.

ACKNOWLEDGMENTS

My daughter, Kelly, for all her help and support. Jerry and Louise Forione who gave me the boot I needed to change my life around. Edward Gillespie- his tales gave me the idea for the creation of this book.

CHAPTER ONE

Seven weeks till Christmas and the city was already lit up like a Christmas tree. Multicolored lights concealed the usual ashen color-- the brightest were on the children's faces. Mom always loved this time of year decorating the tree and their small match box apartment with her three boys. He smiled to himself--she even decorated her wheelchair.

He pulled his old 87 Ford into a parking spot near the older 13th precinct. Red and green lights adorned the entrance. No surprises for him inside; he knew his stocking would be stuffed with suicides this time of year. Ten percent increase they said during the holiday season; bull shit, it was more like thirty. He was greeted by Desk Sergeant Carrick.

"Morning, Ed. Another beautiful day in the ghetto."

"Everyday is a great day in Shangri-La, Fred." He climbed the rickety stairs and headed for Captain Halloran's office. He paused outside the door --brushing back the salt and pepper hair on the top of his 6-foot frame. He adjusted his shirt and pants trying to hide the belt hangover he was getting at age 41. He entered without knocking. The silver-haired man looked up from his desk and a smile graced his round red face.

"How you doing, Ed?"

"Fine, Frank, what's on your mind?"

"I was just thinking of what I could get Barb for Christmas; you know how particular she is."

"She's not that tough. She settled for you."

"That's what I mean. What could I possibly get her after that?"

"What you got for me?"

"New assignment."

"New assignment! We're up to our asses sifting out suicides from homicides this time of year."

"The holidays do bring out the best people."

7

"When I retire, Frank, I'm going to write a book, "Suicide: Get It Right the First Time.""

"There has been a rash of supermarket robberies by a Hispanic group; couple of people killed, several injured. Inspector Toth and the other brains want to put stakeout teams in the high crime areas; you'll be in charge of one of them."

"Who did I draw?"

"Don't know, but you'll find out at the briefing at ten today."

"I know what you can give Barb."

"What?"

"Same thing I gave my ex-wife. A weeks vacation on each one of the 1,000 islands in upper New York State."

Gilespie's 54-year-old friend laughingly said, "Get your sorry ass out of here."

"How's our boys?"

"They're fine."

"Still squeezing the bagpipes?"

"Yes, and no remarks about that; now get."

Homicide Detective, Sergeant Edward Gilespie smiled as he returned to the bullpen --Mom would have loved the big Irishman with the bright blue eyes. He took her South Bronx boy, broke him in on the job and pushed him into night college classes. She would be proud of the youngest of her three boys. He called to Jim Trafton as he reached his desk.

"Yea, what's up, Ed?"

"You're the boss till I get back."

"Where you going?"

"On stakeouts. You guys will have to handle all the kamikaze people without me."

"Wonderful."

"Yea, take care of the guys."

"Will do, Ed. Good luck."

"Thanks."

CHAPTER TWO

She looked around at the various torsos in the room wondering what they were thinking or saying. Homicide Detective Gladys Krazinski was the first female assigned to that division. After several years of fighting the system, she had finally cracked the all male domain--she had reached her goal. Now, she had another problem to face. They discovered she was a lesbian. She spotted Gilespie as he entered the room; when he turned her way she waved to him without thinking. Oh God! *Why did I do that*, she said to herself--she knew why. He was the only one who had been nice to her. Gilespie waved and headed her way.

"Hi, Gladys. Hooked you too?"

"Yes, sounds like it might be interesting."

"Usually it's hours and hours of being bored."

"We did a lot of stings in vice, not stakeouts; this is new to me."

"We will soon here what's up, here comes Inspector Gadgit.."

The squad room of the old 13th was crammed with bodies as Inspector Toth approached the podium --small man, high school grad only. He played politics very well; ass kissin helped also. The gray haired 54- year-old would do anything to make chief before he reached 30 years of service. His repulsive habit in life was cigar smoking; nervously he twisted the cigar in his mouth. His other claim to fame is a hatred of Italians.

"Okay, okay, knock off the bull shit; listen up." He looks down and reads from a prepared statement. "There has been 12 armed robberies of supermarkets by a Hispanic group- three maybe four involved. Two people have been killed; several injured. We are forming stakeout teams. Two from robbery, two from homicide. The senior officer or detective will be in charge of the team. As I call your names please form to my left; pick up your assignment, get acquainted and should you have any questions, see me after the assignments have been given out. Check out your markets this afternoon to get a plan of coverage in place. The stakeouts will start at seven this evening. First team: Sergeant Gilespie, Detectives Hammad, Krazinski and Silverman."

Gilespie picked up the assignment and headed for the back of the room with Krazinski. He thought nice Christmas present. I draw the new broad; at least the other guys are seasoned. He and Krazinski pull some empty chairs together. Hammad joins them. A plain, un-adorned man except for his olive complexion and slight accent--he was born in Iran. He extends his hand to Krazinski.

"Hi, my name's Hammad. My nick's 'Ham' or 'Dam,' what's your's?"

"My name's Gladys Krazinski... friends call me 'Happy Bottom.'"

Hammad laughs loudly and slaps his knee.

"I a.. .I like, Glad-Ass better."

Detective Arnie Silverman joins them--a very good looking man; his problem is he knows it. He is immediately fascinated by the tall woman with the angelic face surrounded by short blonde hair and her hourglass figure. An automatic sits on her hip with a pair of thirty eight's above. Boy, what he is thinking.

"Hi. They call me Silkie, what's your name?"

"I'm Glad." She is interrupted by Hammad.

"Her name's Glad-Ass, Silkie."

"Okay, guys. Knock it off," said Gilespie. "Call her Gladys, that's it."

"Gladys, it's my pleasure to meet you," said Silkie. "Never saw a homicide beauty like you before; how long you at it?"

"Three months."

"How about that," said Hammad. "We got a 90 day wonder here."

"That's enough," said Gilespie. "Let's see what they gave us. Pace Market on south first; you guys know that area?"

"Yeah," Silkie replies, "20 percent old timers, 30 percent black, and 60 percent Hispanic. Ham would fit in there not us."

"You can't add," Jew boy replies. "Ham, that's 110 percent. Besides, I thought when you put your little beanie on you'd fit in any where."

"That's it," said Gilespie. "Leave the ethnic stuff for the United Nations." Ham and Silkie burst into laughter and slapped their hands together.

"What's the joke?" asked Gilespie.

"Silkie and I are partners," replied Ham. "They call us the UN team."

"That's great. Now let's go check out the market. Gladys, you can ride

with me."
    "The lady can ride with me," said Silkie.
    "I wouldn't want to break up such a great team," replied Gilespie.

CHAPTER THREE

Gilespie looked at his watch; no action yet. He and Ham are on the top of a freezer in the rear of the market, which gives them an overview of the entire store. Silkie is behind a stack of empty boxes at the front near the manager's cage. Gladys is pushing a cart around pretending to shop.

"You married, Ed?" asked Ham.

"Was once, didn't work out."

"I got two great kids myself," said Ham.

"I got three, but they're not mine."

"Who they belong to?"

"Long story; watch the store."

"I thank God every day that my kids were born in America."

"Your wife American?"

"Yes, but her parents were Iranian too."

"What made you take this job? Most times it shows you the bad part of America."

"You think this is bad. You should talk to my parents. I took this job to help people. And found out most we deal with don't want help."

"You got that right."

"You work with Glad-Ass before?"

"Not really."

"Word is she's a lezbo."

"I don't give a shit about that as long as she does her job."

"What makes a good looking broad like that turn lezbo?"

"Maybe she ran into too many guys like you and Silkie."

"Nice dig. Take it you like her."

"Are you interested in her or just taking a survey? Either way, just get off it."

"Just curious, but Silkie will find out."

"Silkie?"

"Yeah, that handsome Jew boy has a good line and a way with real ladies man. Once he got stabbed on the job and I went to see h. hospital. One of his broad's was there. Within five minutes two others showed up. Man, was he in deep shit."

"Right now, forget Silkie's love life. Watch the store."

"Just making conversation, Sarge---You see those guys?"

"I'm zeroed in."

Two males had entered the store taking shopping carts. They moved down separate aisles towards the back. One stayed there looking around while the other moved up another aisle towards the front. A third male entered and stood near the front door.

Gilespie whispered into his lapel mike. "Silkie, you see those guys?"

"I see them."

"One's moving up the aisle towards the cage."

"I got him covered."

"Gladys, cover the one standing near the door."

"I'm coming across. I got him."

"Okay, Ham and I are coming up. We'll cover the other guy and your backs."

The male in the back came forward and nodded to the one near the cage. He whipped out a gun and leaned over the cage. "Open the safe! Give me all the money or I'll blow your fucking head off!"

Silkie knocked all the empty boxes down and stepped out with a shotgun. Hearing the noise, the male whipped around to face Silkie.

Silkie said, "Merry Christmas, Mother Fucker!" and put two rounds into him. Gilespie and Ham took the other male down. The male at the door made a move. Gladys fired three rounds from her automatic hitting him. He fell out the door.

Gilespie hollered over to Silkie as Ham cuffed the other male. "Are you okay, Silkie?"

"I'm fine. He ain't."

Gilespie headed outside to check on Gladys. She was standing over the male laying on the sidewalk.

"It's a kid! He's . ..he's just a kid. I...1 shot a kid!"

Gilespie put his arm around here and pulled her away. "Take it easy."

She put her arm around him and laid her head on his shoulder sobbing. "A kid, a dam kid, I. ..I never shot anyone before. Oh God!"

"Pull it together. You had no choice. It was him or maybe one of us."

Ham and Silkie came out of the store joining them. Crime scene moved in and the shooting team separated them and began questioning them separately. Ham, Silkie and Gilespie stood together waiting for Gladys who was still being questioned. Gilespie looked at Silkie and said, "You didn't give that guy a chance to give up his weapon."

Silkie glared back at him. "I don't take no chances; they didn't give the others a chance. You got a fucking problem with that?"

Gladys returned to the group. "They can't find a weapon. I know he had one, they can't find one!"

Silkie moved in and put his arm around her, pulling her close to him. "Take it easy babe, calm down."

She pushed him away, then placed both hands on his chest and shoved him against the building. "Leave me alone!"

Gilespie stepped between them saying, "Take it easy. We are all uptight. Let's get out of here and get a drink, I think we all could use one. We can do all the reports in the morning."

Gladys sobbingly said, "No, Ed. Just take me home." She sat in the car, leaned against the door and stared out the window. Gilespie was thinking, *poor 29-year-old kid. She probably had a fucked up childhood; that's why she was the way she was. Maybe just born to be a man --She was far from a man or woman. Now she just looked like a pile of rubble.* He broke the silence.

"Things will work out okay; don't let it turn you inside out doesn't pay to dwell on things past."

"Guess I wasn't very professional crying and all that."

"You're a human being first. You have emotions and wants just like everyone else. People think cops are heartless. How wrong they are."

"What's going to happen now?"

"They will go over everything ten times, don't worry you'll be okay."

"I know he reached for a gun, where is it?"

Gilespie double parked in front of her apartment.

"Just have yourself a good stiff shot and some sleep." He leaned over and kissed her on the cheek. It startled her and she sat straight up in the seat looking at him.

"I'm sorry. I a . ..just a crazy reaction, I..."

"It's all right, Ed. I'll see you in the morning. Goodnight."

As he pulled away he thought--*What the hell did you do that for, you stupid ass.*

14

CHAPTER FOUR

The next morning comes early when you don't get much sleep. Gladys looked like hell; she probably didn't get any. They were working on their reports when Gilespie was buzzed to come to Captain Holloran's office. Lieutenant Harold Laper of the Internal Affairs Division was seated in the office.

"Ed, you know Lieutenant Laper, don't you?"

"Yes, we met a few times." Gilespie was thinking, *the bastard of the rat squad* as he was called by the men. A blonde-silver toupee sat atop his 6-foot-2 skinny frame. He had a protruding nose--perfect for his job; beady eyes; a pertinacious person--the perfect profile of an IA man.

"The Lieutenant is looking into the shooting last night."

"Routine, as far as I'm concerned, considering the situation,"replied Gilespie.

"Far from routine, Sergeant-- are all the reports done?"

"No. We're working on them now."

"I'll need all your reports as soon as possible. Inspector Toth wants this cleared up before we have any unrest in the area."

"Unrest in the area? What are you talking about?"

"Shooting team found no weapon at the scene. We have a dead 17-year-old that we can't connect to the other two. She shot an innocent kid; the Hispanic community will be up in arms."

"I don't think she would have fired if the kid didn't have a weapon. She's to professional for that; maybe people just need a scapegoat."

"Scapegoat! The woman's got a problem, plus she lost it."

"Problem? What's the problem?"

"You know the problem, Gilespie. Hell, half the department knows what she is."

"What is she, Lieutenant? To me she's just a cop who did her job   and

15

probably saved one of our asses. Her sexual orientation is her business!"

Gilespie jumped up and shoved his chair back, which fell to the floor. His face twisted into a stern look. "You've been on her ass since she was in vice because she wouldn't give you a piece of it! If you dragged me in here to nail that ass you got the wrong boy! I'm leaving."

Captain Halloran jumped to his feet. "Ed, take it easy! Don't make matters worse here."

"He can go, Captain. I don't need him; she fucked herself."

"You better watch your mouth."

"Gilespie, you're not out of the woods yet. You were in charge of that team."

Gilespie stormed out of the office slamming the door behind him and returned to the bullpen.

"Your face is a little red, Ed. They give you a hard time?" asked Silkie.

"Nothing I can't handle coming from that ass hole. Finish up your reports so I can give them to the lovely man. Then we take the rest of the day off-- screw this place."

Gilespie was again buzzed by Captain Halloran.

"Gladys, the Captain wants to see you. Silkie, you'll be after her."

A stark look came over her face as she got up and headed for the office.

"What's going on in there?" asked Ham.

"You know, the routine after a shooting. You get a forced vacation. I want you guys to meet me at Quinn's tavern after we get through all this bull shit. I've got something I want to run by you."

Gladys returned to the group and Silkie headed for the office.

"How did you make out with that bastard?" asked Gilespie.

"Got some time off till they finish with the shooting investigation; he wasn't too nice. Said it didn't look good."

"Don't let him get to you; it will be okay."

"I a... I'm going home Ed." Gladys turned and started walking away.

CHAPTER FIVE

Gilespie decided to walk the few blocks to Quinn's. He was lucky enough to get a parking spot near the precinct. *I've got to convince these guys to help me*, he was thinking. Plying them with drinks wasn't the answer, but he had to get them to check out his gut feeling. Quinn's was an old neighborhood bar that was all Irish years ago; as the area changed so did the clientele. The overcast chilly day hadn't cooled him down, he needed a cool down drink. That fuck Laper would push this thing--the gun was the answer. He entered Quinn's and headed directly for the bar. With the low ceiling the smoke was hanging just like a London fog. He ordered a drink and looked around. Ham and Silkie were seated in a booth near the back; he slipped into the booth next to Ham.

"What's this action?" said Ham. "I thought you were buying."

"I never like to wait for the first one; the offer still stands, I'll pick up the tab."

"What did you want to run by us?" asked Silkie.

"Gladys has a problem brewing."

"This problem wouldn't be IA, would it?" said Ham.

"Not so much IA; it's Laper."

"That prick", said Silkie. "I heard about him."

"I don't like screwing with them people," said Ham. "They can really fuck you up."

"What's this 'we' shit?" said Silkie.

"We're not going to screw with the IA guys--I think the kid had a gun and we're going to find it."

"No gun was found," said Ham. "Where is this mystery gun?"

"Wait a minute, Ham. Let's get this 'we' shit straight; what do you mean by 'we'?" asked Silkie.

"You guys know that area better than anyone. I'd like you to put my gut feeling to work."

"Which is?" asked Ham.

"I think the kid had a gun and someone outside picked it up and split."

"That's a thousand to one shot," said Silkie.

"I think she goofed. In my country women don't do men's jobs. She should change her style. Stay home, have kids."

"What country are you in now, Ham?! America or Iran? The 'she' is not a 'she,' the she is a cop and cops help cops!"

Ham and Silkie looked at each other. They were surprised by Gilespie's outburst.

"Why the savior? You related to her or something?" said Silkie.

"No, and change your line of thought. Look guys, I feel that Laper wants her ass because he couldn't have a piece of it or some other reason. Don't ask me how, but I just know that kid had a gun."

"How could Silkie and I help?"

"You guys know that area better than anyone. Put the word out to your people that we know someone split with the weapon. No guy. No weapon. We will shake up that area so bad they'll think an earthquake hit."

"They're not stupid," said Silkie. "They know we got nothing. Besides, a lot of them would love to see a cop hang."

Gilespie gave them a big smile and leaned back in the booth. "We got somewhere already. Silkie you just said 'cop,' not 'she'."

"I'm on paid leave till they finish up with that shooting bull shit. I've got to watch what I do."

"Maybe we could talk to a few dignitaries and see what happens,"said Ham.

"You sure switched to a bleeding heart fast. Ham, remember what could happen. This isn't an official job, we could wind up in deep shit."

"We haven't done our act in awhile, Silkie. What the hell, it could be fun."

"What do you say, Silkie? You with us?" said Gilespie.

"Fuck it. I had no vacation plans anyway, I'm in."

Gilespie smiled and raised his glass. "It's great to see the UN agree on something. Let's get another round and give me that tab."

Driving home, Gilespie watched the joyful people hustling along the streets. They say this is the time of year people open up with kindness and giving –*Why was he sticking out his neck for her? Was it out of kindness or because it was the right thing to do? Tell yourself the truth,* he was thinking. *You want to get in her pants just like the rest of them. Maybe it was more; he was attracted to her. Get that shit out of your mind.She's just a kid to you.* He entered his apartment, headed straight for the refrigerator, grabbed a can of beer, then on to his favorite chair. This was his habitual routine at day's end. *To call her or not to call her,* he was thinking. The hell with it, *maybe I can make her feel better*--he dialed the number.

"How you doing, Gladys?"

"Okay, I guess. What's going to happen next?"

"Everything's going to be fine, don't worry. I want to pick your brain for a minute or two about who was around you outside the market."

"I'm not up to that right now, Ed"

"It's important. I have a feeling I know where the gun went."

"All I can see is that kid's face."

"Then how about meeting.me for breakfast tomorrow; get some sleep and we can talk then."

"I don't know, Ed."

"Please, Gladys. I think I have the answer. How about Jackie's at eight?"

"Okay, Ed. Goodnight."

"Goodnight."

CHAPTER SIX

Jackie's was a little mom and pop joint--breakfast and lunch only--with great food. Gladys was sitting at a table for two in the middle of the small place. Gilespie slid into the seat opposite her.

"Morning, kid."

"Morning, Ed."

"You got bags; haven't been sleeping, right?"

"Nice compliment to start my day."

"Don't take it wrong, I'm concerned."

The waitress interrupted them. "Two coffees?"

"Yes, please," Gladys replied.

"Are you ready to order?"

"Not yet. Give us a few minutes."

"I don't know if I can eat yet, Ed."

"You have to keep going--he had a gun right?"

"I'm so confused with everything I'm not even sure."

"Take your time. Think back, what did he do?"

"When Silkie hit that one guy, I saw him reach. There was a silver reflection from the light. I assumed gun, maybe I was wrong."

"I don't think you were wrong. After he was hit and fell out the door, what did you do?"

"I froze for a second then headed for the door; he was laying on the sidewalk outside."

"Did you see a gun?"

"I didn't look..a. ..he was just a kid, a young kid."

"Push that aside. Think. Who was around you?"

"Some kids came running up, some men, some women. I can't remember."

"Bring it back in your mind. Just concentrate on the crowd."

"People were running up, that's all I...WAIT!...one...one was running away!"

"Good, now focus on that person."

"Dark clothes, dark cap...a skull cap."

"Anything else?"

"A design on the back of the jacket. I don't know what it was. Green and red a...Yes!...it was green and red."

"Good, now we're getting somewhere. What else can you remember?"

"That's all. ED, what's going to happen to me?" Gladys put her head in her hands and began sobbing.

"Take it easy, kid. Pull yourself together. We have something to work with now."

She looked back up at Gilespie; tears were streaming down her cheeks. "They're all after me, the cops, the people, I'm not a bad person. I'll just resign --I want them all out of my life!"

"Get that out of your mind. We have something to work with now; ten to one that guy ran off with the weapon."

The waitress approached them. "Are you ready to order now?"

"I'm sorry, Ed. I... I can't eat right now."

"Please just bring me the tab."

"Ed, let's just leave. I just want to go home."

"You can't hide in a shell, you have to move on."

Gladys stood up, and dabbed at her eyes with a tissue. "I'm sorry, Ed. I'm leaving." She turned and almost ran out as the people stared at Gilespie.

Gilespie was unaware of the focus on him. He was thinking, *I have to get this information to the UN right away.*

CHAPTER SEVEN

"You really think we should be involved in this thing, Silkie?"

"No, I don't. But that Laper turns my stomach. He's screwed some good cops I knew. I'd like to turn his ass hole inside out."

Ham looked at his partner of two years. Dark curly hair, unblemished face, a perfect muscular body: he could have been a male model or movie star; 33-year-old girls easily fell for him.

"I know you, Silkie. You're thinking that by helping this broad, you'll have a good shot to nail her."

Silkie looked at Ham. Only 31 and getting out of shape. A real family man. He'wondered if he would screw around if he got the chance.

"I'd fuck her in a heart beat, would'nt you?"

"I'm married. I don't think like that. Your mind's always in the gutter."

"I know you too, maybe I'll jump in the sewer with you."

"Silkie, there's Spanish Joe on the corner; park this heap."

They approach Spanish Joe on the corner. His face tightened into a sneer and he shook his head from side to side.

"Joe, how you been doing?" asked Ham.

"Fine, till now. What you guys want?"

"We lost a piece of evidence. You know all, where can we find it?" asked Silkie.

Joe looked at Ham. "What's he talking about?"

"A newly acquired weapon by one of the locals."

"Shit, there's a lot of weapons around here, new and old."

"This one's special. It was picked up for free right off the sidewalk," said Silkie.

"I don't know what you're talking about."

"Joe, it's very important you level with us; especially for your own good," said Ham.

"Why you hassling me? I don't know anything."

"Your booking operation and flea market sales are about to close," said Silkie.

"You guys going to lean on me for nothing."

"As Silkie would say, 'your the yenta in the neighborhood.' Joe, where did the gun go?"

"Damn! I said I don't know what you talking about."

"Let's start with something else; it may jog your memory--you know the dragons, don't you?" asked Silkie.

"Their jackets have a green dragon with red flames coming out of its mouth," said Ham.

"Yeah, that's their colors."

"Good," said Silkie. "Now, which one of them picked up the gun the night of the market robbery?"

"I don't know which one."

"Ah," said Ham, "You know one of then did."

"I didn't say that!"

"You implied that," said Silkie.

"You trying to tell me what I said, I didn't say that."

"Then tell us again," said Ham. "But be very careful. Your license is on the line."

Silkie added, "Think about it, Joe. It's your last shot."

"I don't need no trouble on either end."

"Joe, Joe," Ham said. "You don't know what real trouble is--just tell us what you know and your life goes on without us."

A crowd started to form halfway down the block; they were pointing at them and started to move their way.

"You guys are attracting attention; I don't need no spot light."

"Say the word and we can turn it off in a second," said Silkie.

"Okay, I heard one of the Dragon dudes got a gun from the shooting, but I don't know which one."

As the crowd started to gather around them, Joe started to ease away.

"These guys bothering you, Joe?" one man said.

"No, they're cops. It's okay."

Another shouted out, "Cops are no fucking good, they kill young kids."

Ham held up his hands saying, "Whoa! You people just move on. This is none of your business."

Another male pushed his way to the front. He had been busted by

Silverman before. He shouted out, "Fuck you and your fucking kike Jew bastard friend! Get out of our turf!"

In one swift move, Silkie grabbed him by the front of his jacket and jammed the barrel of his gun under his chin. "What did you say? Say it again, you fucking spic, and see if you finish it."

"Ease up, Silkie. We don't need this. You people bust it up and move away."

Grudgingly Silkie released his grip and shoved the man backwards and he fell to the pavement.

"Get up and get the fuck out of here while you can still walk."

They gingerly made their way back to their vehicle with the crowd a short distance behind. As they pulled away from the curb, they get clobbered with garbage, bricks, a flower pot and anything else the group could get their hands on.

"You scared the shit out me, Silkie. I thought you lost it for sure."

"I'm okay. Just get away from this garbage dump."

CHAPTER EIGHT

Gilespie entered Captain Halloran's office the next morning, laying on his desk was the morning paper.

"You read it?"

"I read it."

"Hell of a mess, Ed. She's in deep shit."

"She needs help, Frank. All those bleeding hearts and anti-cop groups want to hang her. The kid had a gun."

"Shooting team and IA boys concluded there was no gun."

"Laper and his rat squad fucked up the compass so it only pointed to her."

"Speaking of Lieutenant Laper; he called me. Informed me that Captain Russo of the robbery division had two of his men involved in a little tousle yesterday. Seems they were inquiring about a gun taken from the shooting scene-- your name came up as a believer also. Laper wanted to know what YOU guys were doing interfering with an IA investigation. Level with me, Ed. What's going on?"

"The kid had a gun. One of the Dragon's street gang picked it up and split the scene."

"You can prove that?"

"Not yet. That's what we were working on."

"You're not authorized to be working on that--Laper will hang your ass."

"That son-of-a-bitch is looking for revenge and glory because he couldn't make it with Gladys. I did some checking and found out that he fell for a broad and they hooked up for awhile; then she left him. When Gladys went into vice he tried to make it with her, but it was no go. Then he found out that she was a lesbian; since then he's been out to nail her and is after a plain clothes cop by the name of Lloyd Tucker, who he also thinks is gay. Both of them should sue his fucking ass."

"My, you're up on all the social events, Ed. You should write a column."

"I'm no crusader for the gay cause, but he's going out of his way to nail them."

"Let me give you some advise, Ed. It's bad for your career to upset Inspectors and Chiefs. Lay off this thing or you'll wind up with your ass in a vice."

"I'll watch myself, but I know I'm right. Is that it?"

"One more thing, Ed. I hate to do this, but I'm ordering you to drop this investigation of your's. That's official right from Inspector Toth."

Gilespie stood up and gave Halloran a salute. "Aye, aye, Captain."

"Don't be a smart ass, Ed. Lay off it."

"Okay, no problem." Gilespie left the office.

Halloran thought, *that stubborn Irishman won't drop it. I hope he doesn't get caught in the cross fire.*

Gilespie returned to his desk and called Silverman at home. "How's the UN doing?"

"We split. Remember, I'm on paid leave."

"Do you guys know the leader of the Dragons?"

"Yeah, Jose Bacardi. They call him 'Rum'."

"Can you guys get word to him that I want to meet with him?"

"Spanish Joe could contact him, but that means going back into that area and that's a no, no."

"Can't let this die out, I need one more shot."

"We can't go back into that area again. Captain Russo ordered us to leave everything to the rat squad."

"Please do me this last favor."

"Look, Ed. Those bastards hate us, plus the Captain said lay off. That's it. In fact, you almost had another murder to investigate yesterday."

"Please, Silkie. All you have to do is get word to this 'Rum.' I'll give you my home phone number. Tell him to call me; he can pick the spot and I'll come alone. I need this one last shot for her."

"I don't know, Ed. Let me run this past Ham."

"Tell him I'll have him deported if he doesn't do it."

"I will. That should piss him off."

Gilespie returned to completing his reports; 'shit sheets' he called them. He wondered how Gladys was doing. *Maybe I should call her.* He picked up the phone then dropped it back in the cradle. *Not the right time, but I've got to talk to her about my problem.*

CHAPTER NINE

Gilespie and Krazinski sat in his vehicle near a factory by the river.

"Do you think they will show, Ed?"

"Will soon know. It's almost six."

"I'm scared, Ed. They think I killed that kid for nothing."

"Wrong, they got the gun he had plus he's not one of their's. They don't do holdups--Gladys, there's something I have to tell you."

"Not more bad news I hope."

"It's . . . I don't know how to say this, but bear with me I may mess it up."

"Look! Ed, there's a van pulling in."

They watched the beat-up gray van pull in; it stopped a few yards from them. Two males got out and looked around, then approached their vehicle. Ed and Gladys got out of the car; one male stood on each side of them. One then waved to the van and two more males got out and approached them. The smaller of the two was wearing a red and green bandanna. He had a dark complexion, black hair and a mustache to match. There was a very visible scar running down his neck. By his walk he fit the small man syndrome--*he is Rum*, Gilespie said to himself.

"I'm Rum. Thought you said alone." He nodded towards Gladys.

"I like companionship while I wait," Gilespie replied.

Rum looked Gladys up and down, then smiled revealing some missing teeth and one gold one. "Understandable. Talk."

"How would you like to be man of the year in the community?" asked Gilespie.

"Will my picture be on *Peoples* mag or a mug shot?"

"Can't promise the first, but the second won't happen."

"What you laying out here?"

"Plain and simple deal. Your man with the gun turns himself in, makes a statement and walks away; no charges."

"That's a good fairy tale; never heard that one. Plus who are you to make promises?"

"I'm a little guy, but big enough to back up what I say. None of your boys was involved in that market job but one of them did walk away with a gun. Take a good look at this lady. You going to let her hang and your playground burn over a gun?"

Rum looked at Gladys. "You blew the kid away?"

Gladys gave him a cold hard stare. "A kid is not a kid when he has a weapon," she replied.

"I don't know what you're talking about one of my boys being involved."

"Okay, why don't you look into it. I'm sure you'll find out the right answer to the problem. You would gain a new image if you helped us out," said Gilespie.

"Help cops out! The only times you helped us out, was out a third floor window!"

"Think about it, Rum. You would be number one in the playground."

"I like the threads we wear now. I wouldn't look good in saintly robes. What else you got? I'm running late on my appointments."

"That's it, Rum. I know you don't want any trouble."

"Trouble! You pushing me, man! I don't like being pushed."

"No, but speaking of pushing, I once pushed a Mac truck from here to Florida."

"You're a smart ass, but I'm going to check this out."

"When will you get back to me?"

"When I'm ready." Rum and his two boys turned around and walked away.

"What do you think he will do, Ed?"

"I don't know, but I"m sure he's got the answer."

"I hope he does."

"How did you make out with Internal Affairs?"

"Not good. I overheard one guy say something about a manslaughter charge."

"That's bull shit talk, don't pay any attention to it."

"What was it you were going to tell me before, Ed?"

"Nothing."

"It wasn't important?"

"No a....not important. We have to hope that Rum sees the light; if not we have to do it the hard way."

"Ed, something's wrong. I can tell. What is it?"

"Nothing's wrong. We'll clear you one way or the other."

"I sense something's wrong. It's not about Rum. What is it?"

"I think I'm in love with you. I wanted...Damn it! That's not the way to explain it."

"Ed, I don't know what to say. I'm astounded. I...I never intended to...if.. if I led you to believe I...didn't.."

"I'm sorry. Forget it, Gladys. Forget I said it."

Gilespie pulled up in front of her apartment.

"Ed, we have to talk. Come up, I'll make some coffee."

"Please, Gladys. Not now. Goodnight."

"Ed, please."

"Please go. I've embarrassed myself enough."

Gladys got out and stood on the sidewalk. Gilespie pulled away saying to himself, *You stupid bastard. You just made a royal ass out of yourself.*

Gladys entered the building and climbed the stairs to her apartment. She thought, *I like him as a friend. What did I do to make him think it was more than that? God, I have enough problems already.*

CHAPTER TEN

Gilespie sat at his desk scanning the headlines:

RIOT IN HISPANIC COMMUNITY--What started out as a peaceful demonstration in this normally quiet community turned ugly. Chants of 'Killer Cops' and 'Kid Killers' soon pushed the crowd into a frenzy. One officer was seriously injured, several others were treated for cuts and burns. Six persons were arrested; 18 others required medical attention. One Police vehicle was burned. The demonstration was to demand justice for the shooting of an unarmed youth during the robbery of a supermarket several days ago...

Gilespie was interrupted by the phone. "Homicide, Sergeant Gilespie."

"Ed, it's all over TV, the papers! What's going to happen?"

"Gladys! A.. .just a bunch of trouble makers; that's not the real people."

"I'm worried they all want to hang me, the people, the papers, the cops. They all want to hang me."

"Calm down and take it easy. What happened isn't your fault."

"Did you hear from Rum?"

"No. About last night..."

"Do you think he will call?"

"Maybe.. a....yes, I think he will. About last night...I..."

"Yes, we have to talk. What's going to happen with my situation? You've seen this before."

"Don't worry, I'll help you all I can."

"Help me! Then it is bad."

"DAMN IT! Gladys, stop reading doom and gloom into this thing...." He was then interrupted by Captain Halloran. "Hold on."

"Ed, they just found Officer Mario Vazzano DOA. You and Trafton take it. Here's the address."

"Okay. Gladys, I've got a call. Sorry to cut you off, I'll call you back later."

CHAPTER ELEVEN

Trafton was out; he left word for him to meet at the crime scene and hit the bricks solo. 520 South East tenth street was already blocked by other police vehicles. He just left his car behind one of them. Entering the old tenement building he proceeded to the second floor; entering a small front apartment. Crime scene was already on the job. Head Technician George Sikora was in the kitchen standing near Vazzano's body.

"George, what's the story?"

"Two in the chest from a small caliber weapon; definitely not a suicide. Did you know him?"

"No, heard the name somewhere."

"No signs of forced entry or a struggle and from the looks of things nothing seems to be disturbed."

"Meaning he knew the person."

"Who found him?"

"Lady across the hall; patrol is talking to her know."

"Thanks, George. I'll get out of your way for now." Gilespie slipped on a pair of plastic gloves and headed for the bedroom. Nothing was in disarray; bed was made, everything seemed to be proper; neat freak he thought. He started going through some papers on a small desk in the corner--one caught his eye. It was from Lieutenant Laper. Please be advised that you are to report to my office on Tuesday, November 2nd to discuss a matter that has been brought to my attention. That was eight days ago--*Laper in action again,* thought Gilespie. He folded it up and slipped it in to his pocket. Nothing intrigued him further; he returned to the kitchen.

"George, when you get all the shit sheets together get them to me. I'm going to do a little canvassing."

"Okay, Ed."

Gilespie headed for the apartment across the hall. He was about to knock on the door when Patrol Sergeant Al Williams came out.

"Hi, Ed."

"Hi, Al. Get anything?"

"Not much. The woman said she heard talking late last night after midnight; no shots. When she was leaving this morning she noticed the door ajar. Said he walked every morning and thought he forgot to shut it. She called his name a few times and when he didn't answer, she pushed the door open. Saw him on the floor, ran back to her place and called 911. That's it."

"Talk to any of the other tenants yet?"

"No."

"You finish up this floor. I'll take the top floor and have one of your boys hit the first floor."

The canvass of the building turned up nothing. Gilespie talked to some people next door and across the street, but they could add nothing. Driving back to the precinct, Gilespie was thinking, *I wonder what Laper wanted him for. I'll have to check that out along with hangouts and friends* --damn, Trafton never did show UP ?? He filled Captain Halloran in, except for one thing: Laper's letter. He would take care of that bastard. Then he received a phone call from a good friend, Detective Vinnie Carbone, assigned to the West Homicide Division. They had become close after working on a serial killer case a few years back.

"Vinnie, you old bastard, how are you?"

"Fine and you?"

"Good, you just cheered me up. I hope this is a social call."

"Both. Could you meet me at Bernie's tonight for a couple?"

"Don't know. Right now I've got one working."

"I'll be there around six. If you can't make it call."

CHAPTER TWELVE

Bernie's tavern, a long time cops hangout with extraordinary police items and pictures from all over the world. The bubble gum light rack taken from an older police vehicle is mounted behind the bar; the revolving lights are annoying. Gilespie likes them because when they don't bother him anymore he knows he had enough to drink. He spotted Carbone in the middle of the long hardwood bar. Vinnie got up to greet him and gave him a big hug. He was a short, stocky, weight-lifter with crew cut hair; a Marine's Marine. He had five kids at age 37 with another on the way. Vinnie was also a hot-blooded Italian who saved Gilespie's life at one time.

"How's the wife and kids, Vinnie?"

"Fine, Ed. Heard a cop named Vazzano bought the ticket."

"Yeah, I got the case."

"Any suspects yet?"

"No. I found a letter from the rat bastard in his apartment. Could be he was into something."

"You mean Laper?"

"Yeah."

"This is something: That's who I wanted to talk to you about."

"Me?"

"Yeah, word is you're on a crusade for Krazinski and Tucker. My buddy in IA filled me in and wanted to tell you that Laper is looking into you too."

"That fuck!"

"I agree. My partner and I got caught up in the little riot last night. Tucker was the cop who was beaten by the mob."

"What the hell happened?"

"They called for assistance from any units in the area. My partner and I were returning from an investigation; we responded. There was confusion at first, then we established a line of containment. Laper was there giving

33

orders."

"Laper? Where were the patrol commanders?"

"Busy elsewhere. Suddenly, a guy threw a molotov cocktail at a patrol car; Tucker broke ranks and went after him. Laper kept hollering not to break ranks. Tucker grabbed the guy and got him to the ground. The crowd then jumped him. Laper kept hollering not to break ranks, hold the line. When we saw the beating he was taking, my partner and I, plus a uniform guy broke ranks. We got him out of there; he was in bad shape." Laper threatened to put us on report; I don't know if he did."

"The fucking bastard! He left the kid out to dry."

"You got it. My buddy in IA also said he thinks Laper is double dirty."

"How's that?"

"He believes he's shaking down dirty cops and not turning them in."

"I wouldn't put anything past that prick."

"As they say, Ed, now you know the rest of the story."

"Laper is leaning real hard on Gladys. Rumor is that he's pushing the DA to indict her on manslaughter charges. I got a squeal that the kid had a gun, a gang member picked it off the sidewalk and split with it. Poor kid; she's going through hell. She doesn't deserve that; she's a good cop and a beautiful person in many ways."

"What I gather, Ed, is I think you have a...shall we say a fondness for this woman."

"NO! I'm just trying to help out a cop."

"Ed, I've know you for years. I can tell by your talk and actions there's more then just help involved here."

Gilespie takes another sip from his drink; he looks at Vinnie.

"It shows?"

"It shows, Ed."

"You're a good detective, Vinnie. No one else saw it."

"I bet they have, but said nothing."

"What can I do, Vinnie? She's starting to grow on me."

"Take some vacation time or get your Captain to transfer her to another division."

"I just don't know what to do. I think I'm falling in love with her."

"Move on, Ed. When your old lady took off with that guy you were a basket case. I'd hate to see you if it were a woman."

Vinnie then realized what he said. Gilespie shoved his glass back; it fell behind the bar. He stood up and glared at Vinnie.

"I'm sorry, Ed. I didn't mean..."

"Vinnie, you're a bastard for throwing that in my face."

"I'm sorry for putting it that way, but you know it's a long shot that it would work."

Gilespie sat back down as the bartender replaced his drink and stared straight ahead.

"Ed, look..."

"Don't say anymore! End of subject!"

They sat in silence for a few minutes; Vinnie broke it. "I've got to split, Ed. I'm sorry...I a...I wish you well."

"MERRY CHRISTMAS TO YOU TOO!"

Vinnie got up; hesitated for a second then turned and walked away. Gilespie muttered to himself, "Son-of-a-bitch, I didn't need that."

CHAPTER THIRTEEN

The Dragons gathered in their club house, which is the basement under the candy store. They were discussing a problem which had just come to light. Hector Lopez, a young dragon was talking to Rum. "What you want me to do, Rum?"

"You sure that old hag turned you in?"

"Yeha, she's the goody-goody type. She also told my mother."

"Fuck, this screws up my plans. Your sure on this?"

"Yeah, she told me she told the cop at the riot. He said he knew me and would take care of it. You want me to split?"

"No. You're going to have to turn yourself in with the gun. Only after I make a deal with that fucking cop. Nothing will happen to you. I want you to stay at Angel's till this is done. Don't hit the streets or go anywhere, they're probably looking for you."

"Anything you say, Rum."

Gilespie had fallen asleep in his favorite chair when the phone woke him from his drunken stupor. "Hello."

"Did I fuck up your sleep, man?"

"Who is this?"

"Your favorite drink, Rum."

"Rum! How are you doing?"

"I'm doing good. You don't sound to good."

"I was out celebrating my divorce."

"You straight enough to listen?"

"Sure, shoot."

"I understand you know who are boy is."

Gilespie was confused and hesitated for a few seconds. "Could be."

"Yeah, well, you ain't got him yet, but I'm going to float you a deal."

"Pour."

"I want a meet, but I want it with some big boys not just you."

"Such as?"

"Chiefs and the DA, people who have the final word."

"May take a day or two to set that up depending on their schedules."

"Yeah, I'm busy too. Be at the old little league field near the bridge at six tomorrow night; that's it."

The line went dead. Gilespie said to himself, up *What a time for this to happen when I'm all fucked up.* He fumbled through his phone book looking for Captain Halloran's home phone number. He glanced at the clock, damn near 3 a.m. Shit. Oh well. He spotted another number and stared at it. Halloran and Rum can wait till morning; he dialed the number. It rang several times, but then someone answered.

"Hello?..."

"Rhonda, how's it going?"

"ED?"

"Yeah, who else?"

"It's after three in the morning."

"I need to talk to you, my good friend."

"Blond or brunette this time?"

"Suppose it's a redhead."

Rhonda and Gilespie had a strange off on relationship over a few years. He cared for her, but drinking, age difference, plus other problems kept the cement on both sides from drying into a solid block.

"Whatever color. It's going to have to wait. I've got to be at work at seven."

"Won't take long. I just need a little advice."

"NO, Ed. You're drunk and your short stories when you're in that shape turn into novels. Call me tomorrow if you remember you called me tonight. Good morning."

CHAPTER FOURTEEN

Gilespie decided to take the subway to work the next morning. Driving in was getting to be a pain in the ass. Halfway there he was sorry he made that decision; the shake rattle and roll of the subway car wasn't the right music for his hangover. He was still thinking of what Vinnie had said along with the talks with Rum and the Rhonda call. The latter was a bad move, but he would have to call her back. He entered Captain Halloran's office and dropped into the chair in front of his desk.

"My, don't we look like the grim reaper this morning."

"Good and bad night, Frank. Got a good phone call, but punished myself for it."

"YOU got a break in Vazzano's case?"

"No. The Dragon King wants to make a deal, but want's some big boys present. I voted for you and Stanton."

"Vazzano's case is number one on the list; that's a cop killing in case you forgot."

"I didn't. Trafton can handle it. There isn't much to run with right now. This can clear up the Gladys thing."

"What's the pitch?"

"He'll turn over the guy and the gun for some concessions.'

"What are they?"

"Don't know. He wants to meet tonight at six."

"You want me to go with you while you disregard Toth's and my orders? You've got a pair of balls, Ed."

"Yeah, Stanton too."

"Let's all hold hands and jump into the shit bowl you created."

"Frank, this can clear Gladys; he admitted he's got the guy and the gun. One more thing. He said we know who the guy is. You got anything on that?"

"No, but maybe IA does."

"I don't think so."

"You're stepping on their toes."

"Frank, please give it a shot; my gut tells me it's right."

"Tell you what I'll do. Run all this by Stanton; if he okays it, I run with it, but I don't like it."

Gilespie contacted District Attorney John Stanton, an old friend who he worked many cases with in the past. Using his Irish persuasion, Stanton agreed to take a shot at it.

CHAPTER FIFTEEN

"Thanks for going along with this, guys. I know it will work."

"He's going to have the kid, here?"asked Halloran.

"I have to talk to that kid; he's the whole key." said Stanton.

"We'll soon know, guys. There's the ballpark up ahead."

Rum and two of his big boys were already there.

"Rum, this is District Attorney Stanton and Captain Frank Halloran."

They extend their hands to Rum; he waves them away. "We shake after a deal, not before."

"You got the kid here?" asked Gilespie.

"He's around. What I want, Mr. DA, is that the kid doesn't get charged with anything. Two, none of the people who jumped the cop get arrested. Three, which is most important, the cops ease up on our business operations. Fourth, I want it all in writing. Only then do you get the kid and the gun."

"As to number one, that's easy. The kid produces the gun and gives us a statement, no charges. Number two is a serious offense. An assault on a police officer can't be pushed aside."

Rum's face twisted into a scowl. "You guys always look the other way when the cops beat the shit out of us. If it's a one way street you got no deal."

"I'm sorry," said Stanton. "It's a serious matter and can't be pushed aside."

Rum gave him a cold stare then turned to walk away.

"Wait!" said Gilespie. "If we talk to Tucker, John, I'm sure he will understand what's at stake here and go along with us."

"Even so, Ed. It would be a tough sell."

"You can just let the case sit for awhile; things get forgotten and fade way. It's been done before."

"Okay, we'll see. Now, what's these businesses you're talking about?"

"Let's say we meet our needs through gaming and escort service; just enough to meet our needs..."

"Both could be against the law if run improperly."

"We run them properly and we don't need no heat, even this time of year."

"I can't promise you no heat, I don't control the furnace."

"Both are considered victimless crimes," said Gilespie. "No complaints, no action."

"Put it this way," said Halloran, "we won't go out of our way to   nail you. No complaints, no action. That's the best I can offer you."

"No heat, unless we screw up; I can buy that," said Rum. "Looks like we got a deal."

"Rum, you have to understand one thing," said Stanton. "There are certain things that can't be put in writing. You just have to take our word."

Rum gives them a big smile and extends his hand to them.

"First we all shake. That's good, now I will take your word. However, if your word should be no good we have this." Reaching into his pocket, he produced a tape recorder; hit a switch an played back part of their conversation. "You see, gentleman. I'm not as dumb as you think I is. Joey go get the kid." Joey returned in a few minutes with the kid. He was carrying a small paper bag.

"Hector, you go with these gentleman and tell them everything; nothing will happen to you."

"Anything you say, Rum."

"Mr. G, don't forget a good plug for the Dragons."

"What about all the unrest?" asked Gilespie.

"Word will go out tonight; it will be over."

Rum and his big boys walked away laughing, slapping each other on their backs.

CHAPTER SIXTEEN

Gilespie, Halloran and Stanton stand outside the interrogation room looking through the glass at Hector Lopez.

"How about that bastard recording our conversation," said Gilespie.

'That's a no sweat," said Stanton. "He can't use that for anything. It will prove he interfered with an investigation and had evidence related to a crime. He is as dumb as he thinks he is; let's go talk to our boy."

Stanton placed the gun that was in the bag in front of Hector.

"This is the weapon you took that night?"

"Yeah."

"Please tell me how you obtained it."

"I was across the street from the market when I hear shots. I ran across the street to see what was happening and I hear more shots. This dude falls out the door onto the sidewalk. He dropped the gun and it slid across the sidewalk towards the curb. I picked it up and ran, that's it."

"Why did you take it?"

"You can always use a gun in my area for protection."

"You new a female cop was in trouble; why didn't you come forward before?"

"Ain't my problem, cops don't worry about me."

"Why did you come forward now?"

"Because, Rum said it was okay. Besides, Mrs. Hernandez turned me in anyway."

"Who is Mrs. Hernandez?"

"A friend of my mother's; she saw me take the gun."

"Who did she turn you into?"

"You guys."

"The police?"

"Yeah."

"When did she turn you in?"

"The night the cop got beat up. She told one of them."

"You sure she turned you in?"

"Yeah, she's a goody-goody church lady and all that."

"Hector, after your statement as recorded is typed up and after you have read it, will you sign it?"

"Yeah."

"Hector, do you know where Mrs. Hernandez lives?" asked Gilespie.

"Same building as me, apartment six."

Hector was released; Gilespie, Halloran and Stanton continued to talk in the interrogation room.

"Krazinski will be cleared, which I'm glad of," said Stanton.

"I want to find out who Mrs. Hernandez talked to," said Gilespie.

"I'm interested also. Check on that, Ed."said Halloran.

"What do you think of my shit bowl now, Frank?"

"It still has an odor to it, Ed."

CHAPTER SEVENTEEN

"Mrs. Hernandez, I'm Detective Sergeant Gilespie. I'd like to ask you a few questions about Hector Lopez."

"That boy, he gives his mother fits. Is he in trouble again?"

"Did you see him near the market the night of the attempted robbery?"

"Yes, I told the policeman he took the robber's gun."

"When did you tell the policeman he took the gun?"

"The night they had all that trouble."

"Do you know his name?"

"No. He was some kind of officer; giving orders so I told him. Tall, thin, he was wearing a suite with a gold badge."

"What color hair did he have?"

"Light blond, I think."

"What exactly did you tell him?"

"I told him I saw Hector Lopez pick up the robber's gun and run away."

"What did he say?"

"He said he knew him and would take care of it and thanked me."

"Do you remember anything else about him, anything at all?"

"No. Only he had a funny type nose. Is there a problem?"

"No problem. This is just a routine we have to go through. If I showed you some pictures do you think you could pick him out?"

"I think so."

"Would it be okay if I stopped back later and showed you some photos?"

"Yes. Is that lady policeman all right?"

"She's fine. I want to thank you for your time. I'll be back a little later." Gilespie returned to the precinct: he was a happy man. Mrs. Hernandez described Lieutenant Laper; he is sure of it. He entered Captain Halloran's office and couldn't wait to blurt out what he believes. Halloran, however, got the first word in.

"Got squared away with Gladys this morning. Everything is going to be fine. She'll be back to work tomorrow."

"That's great, but I wanted to make that phone call."

"Don't worry she knows who saved her ass."

"They give out a press release yet?"

"No."

"When they do, don't forget to give the Dragons a little credit."

"Yeah, but I don't like that little worm."

"You're not going to like this either. I spoke to Mrs. Hernandez. Based on the description she gave me, she spoke to Laper."

"Laper! Are you sure?"

"Fits Laper; gold badge and all. I've got personnel pulling his file photo and half a dozen sommeliers. We'll see if she can pick him out. Does he know Gladys is cleared?"

"He should. He's in IA. If it's him I can't understand why he didn't turn it in and follow up on it."

"Well, let me finish up on this and see if I can clear it one way or the other."

"Contact me as soon as you know, Ed."

"Will do, Frank."

CHAPTER EIGHTEEN

Gilespie had shown the photos to Mrs. Hernandez. She picked out Laper's photo, stating she was positive he was the one she spoke to. Returning once again to the precinct, Gilespie was overjoyed and couldn't wait to put his report together. *I'm really going to shove this one up your ass, Laper,* he thought. He hurriedly put his report together then entered Captain Halloran's office.

"Here it is, Frank. All in a nice neat package. His ass is grass."

"Is she positive it was him she spoke with?"

"Yeah, she's sure. I don't have any sorrow for the bastard as biased as he was."

"Don't be so overjoyed. He is a cop. Did you forget that?"

"This guy wasn't a cop's cop; he deserves to be screwed."

Halloran started reading Gilespie's report then dropped it on his desk and removed his glasses. "You've got a real push in here. You know better than that."

"What's wrong?"

"You know damn well what's wrong! You can't mention the harassment of Gladys and Tucker in here. It has nothing to do with the issue at hand."

"I want IA to know that's the reason he didn't turn in the squeal on the gun."

"That's for IA to investigate or Krazinski or Tucker to press, not you; now rewrite it."

"Okay, but I want his ass."

"You! Who the hell are you now? Judge and jury. Get off it! Now, out of here and rewrite it."

Gilespie was a little frustrated, but said nothing and returned to his desk. He received a pleasant surprise as Gladys walked into the bullpen.

"Welcome home, kid."

"I wouldn't call it home. I got excited, couldn't stay home. It's like ten tons of weight just fell off my back. I wanted to thank you, Captain Halloran, and the UN team for believing in me."

"Never doubted you for a minute, kid. Now that that's been thrown out the window, we can start the party."

"Party, what party?"

"The Laper hanging party. I've got that bigots ass nailed to the wall. He never turned in the squeal on the gun."

"What do you think will happen to him?"

"After all this, they will can his ass."

"You're really happy about this."

"Aren't you?"

"I have mixed emotions abut it. Knowing your career is over after all these years would devastate me. Maybe it's too harsh."

"To harsh! That's what he was trying to do to you. You never cease to amaze me, kid."

"I know his reasoning; he was frustrated and upset because of me."

"YOU! What are you talking about?"

Gladys looked around the bullpen then leaned over Gilespie's desk. "There's something I never told you or anyone, maybe I should have. The woman that left Laper became my lover."

Gilespie pushed back in his chair, his mouth dropped open; there was a blank stare on his face.

"I believe that's the reason he did the things he did. The affair didn't last long. It's all over now; I guess he never forgot it. I should have told you sooner. I'm sorry."

"That's a... that doesn't make any difference; what he did was wrong regardless."

Captain Halloran approached them.

"Ed, you guys take this. Tucker's been found DOA!"

CHAPTER NINETEEN

Gilespie and Krazinski arrived at Tucker's apartment building. A patrolman was standing by a patrol vehicle; he was talking to a male sitting in the back seat. They approached them.

"Gilespie and Krazinski, Homicide. What have we got here?" said Gilespie.

"I'm Patrolman Lambros; this is Mr. Biden. He found the vic."

"Mr. Biden, did you see anyone around when you found Mr. Tucker?" asked Gilespie.

"No."

"What?"

"No, I a . ..I just ran out and called 911."

"What is your relationship to Mr. Tucker?"

"I'm... I'm just a friend. My God, this is terrible; I'm very upset."

"Lambros, please get a full statement from Mr. Biden. Then you can turn him loose."

The crime scene unit arrived as Gilespie and Krazinski entered the apartment. Tucker was on the floor in the kitchen.

"You okay for this, Gladys? You knew him too."

"I have to be."

They studied the area as crime scene unit moved in.

"Looks like two in the chest, small caliber weapon, no signs of a struggle," said Gilespie.

A crime scene unit man approached them. "You guys done yet?"

"For now," Gilespie said. "Do your thing."

"Wait! Ed, look at the base molding near him. There's blood on it, but it's outside the splatter sequence. They both studied this for a few minutes.

"What do you make of it, Ed?"

"Looks like a letter, then trails off."

"Ed, his right hand is in a fist except for his first finger that has blood on it. He was trying to write something in his own blood."

"I think you're right. You guys make sure you get some good shots of that from every angle. Good eye, Gladys. I might have missed that."

"So would I, but I had to look away from Tucker."

They and the patrolmen started a canvass of the building. A short, older woman with silver hair and an Irish brogue you could cut with a knife, responded to Gladys's knock.

"Hello, I'm Detective Gladys Krazinski. I'd like to ask you a few questions."

"Yes."

"Did you hear any gun shots last night or early this morning?"

"No."

"Did you hear any noises, voices or see anyone around?"

"No, I mind me own business."

"Did you know your neighbor, Mr. Tucker?"

"No, I mean yes, just to say hello, good-bye."

"Did you know that he was a police officer?"

"Yes."

"He was shot to death last night or early this morning."

"GOD!" (She blessed herself.)

"What's your name?"

"Noreen, Noreen Kelly."

"That medallion you're wearing, is that the Immaculate Conception Medal?"

"Why, yes it is."

"Mother Mary wouldn't like it if you lied to me. Would she?"

"No. No, she wouldn't."

"I believe that you're not telling me the truth. It's very important that you tell me the truth or it may come back to haunt you."

"I a. ..come in, come in please."

Gladys entered the apartment as the woman looked up and down the hall then closed the door. "I don't want no trouble. I mind me own business. I'm no busy body."

"What do you know, Noreen?"

"Like I said, I ain't no busy body, but I stayed up late last night watching TV. About 11:30 p.m. I heard loud voices coming from Mr. Tucker's apartment. I couldn't understand what they were saying, but someone shouted about 'you people are ruining everything'."

"Can you remember anything else, anything at all?"

"I heard someone leave, so I peeked out me window and saw a man walking away up the street."

"Can you describe him, what he looked like or what he was wearing?"

"A white man, short, wearing a dark trench coat."

"Can you remember anything else?"

"No and that's the truth, I swear."

"Here's my card, Noreen. If you should recall anything at all please call me. Mother Mary will be happy you told me the truth."

"Blessed be God."

Gladys rejoined Gilespie and the patrolman. "You get anything, Ed?"

"Nothing. No one heard any shots either."

"Silencer."

"Probably. No struggle and nothing disturbed; he knew the person. This thing is matching Vazzano's murder; we'll check with Trafton to see what he's got going and compare notes."

"The woman I interviewed said she heard loud voices about 11:30 p.m., looked out the window and saw a short white male walking up the street."

"Well, guys, let's start canvassing the neighborhood and see if we can come up with anything else."

CHAPTER TWENTY

Early next morning at the 13th Precinct, Gilespie was going over reports and his coffee stained notes. Gladys came in and sat down in front of his desk.

"Get any sleep?" asked Gilespie.

"Not much, and you?"

"A little."

"You didn't go home, did you, Ed?"

"No."

"I could tell. Your deodorant isn't working."

"All they had here to use was janitor in the drum. Forget the compliments; let's go over what we got."

"Okay."

"Estimated time of death is between 9 p.m. and 1 a.m. Autopsy is scheduled for 10 a.m. today. Based on the entrance wounds. crime boys feel it was a small caliber weapon, possibly a 32-caliber. No signs of a struggle and apparently nothing of value was taken."

"What about that scrawling on the baseboard?"

"Got some shots of that here some place. Here they are."

They sat and studied these for a few minutes. Then Gladys said, "Looks like a line coming down, then off to the right, a blob, then it trails off to the floor. I don't know what to make of it?"

"Me either."

"I think he was trying to write something, but what?"

"Okay, the canvassing didn't produce anything except for what you got from the old lady."

"What about prints?"

"Nothing on that yet. Slugs will be checked after the autopsy for sommeliers and my good old gut feeling tells me they will match the one taken from Vazzano."

"What's are starting point, Ed?"

"We talk to all his friends, then find out what his haunt's were."

"What's the motive?"

"I don't know. Maybe a jilted love, heated discussion over something and the person flipped. I don't know."

"If the two cases connect, maybe a hatred of cops."

"Can't come up with that theory right now I . ..WAIT! Hate, that's it. Hate. Let me see those photos again. Look at this, Gladys. The blood smear on the baseboard. It comes down then drifts to the right, then starts up with that little dab almost in the middle then falls off to the floor. I'll bet he was trying to make an 'L' then an 'A.' That's it. He was trying to spell 'LA.' Get it? He was trying to spell 'Laper'."

"Wait, Ed. I think your reading a little to much into this."

"My gut tells me it is; he hated you and Tucker. Hate, that's our motive."

"What about Vazzano's murder, how does that fit in?"

"Word was he was shaking bad cops down, maybe Vazzano was one of them."

"I still think you're moving too fast on this one, Ed."

"Got to find out where he was last night. Damn! Personnel won't open till 9 a.m. I need his address."

"I know his address."

"YOU?"

"Remember, I used to live with his ex."

"Where is it?"

"Nantucket Apartments in the Village."

"Come on. Let's go."

"Ed, I still think you're pushing this too fast."

"Then I'll go it alone."

"Okay, I'll go but I..."

"I know, let's go."

Gilespie and Krazinski arrived at Laper's apartment; Gilespie was really pumped up. He rang the bell and knocked several times to no avail.

"Stay here. I'll get the Super."

"Ed, you're not going to."

"Yes, I am. Don't say a word."

Gilespie returned with the Super who unlocked the door then left.

"Ed, we can't do this. It's illegal."

"He's got my card, I'll take the rap."

"What are you looking for?"

"Anything that will connect him with anything. You take the kitchen. I'll start in the bedroom."

"I don't like this, Ed. This is wrong."

"Then wait outside. I'll do the whole fucking place myself."

Reluctantly, Gladys started looking around. Neatly and carefully they searched the entire apartment and came up with nothing. They stood in the kitchen.

"There's got to be something here, I know there's something here," said Gilespie.

"I wish I knew what this something was. What law are we going to break next?"

"Let me think; did you check the fridge?" Gilespie opened the freezer and started going through it.

Gladys said, "You hungry? This one doesn't feel right."

Gilespie ripped open the box and found a sealed packet inside. He ripped it open, finding a list of names with numbers next to them. He studied this for a minute; then smiled.

"BINGO! One of the names on this list is Vazzano's."

"You won't be able to use that in court, Ed."

"No, but if we get one of these guys on this dirty bag list to open up. He's screwed."

Gilespie and Krazinski returned to the Super's apartment, thanking him for his cooperation.

"Do you know where Mr. Laper is?"

"No, he said he was taking a few days off. Is there some sort of trouble?"

"No. No trouble at all. You have my card, tell him to call me as soon as he returns."

"I certainly will."

"Thank you."

CHAPTER TWENTY-ONE

They were seated in Captain Halloran 's office giving him an update.

"Are we headed for a dead end on both cases here, or what?"

"Not really, Frank. I have a suspect in mind, but Gladys isn't a believer."

"Who would that be?"

"Laper."

"LAPER! You got something substantial I hope. Don't give me that gut crap on this one."

"Laper was after Gladys and Tucker for various reasons; Vazzano, he was shaking down and he was about to turn him in. That was his motive there. Hatred was the motive regarding Tucker.."

"Can you prove any of this?"

"Most of it."

"Most of it doesn't fly. First, your biased reports on Laper, now this. I think you're just obsessed with getting him and I know the reason why. What do you think of this, Gladys?"

"I know Laper is dirty; something I didn't know before. I can't fathom him killing anyone for any reason. He loves himself too much to end his life that way."

"Woman's point of view, Frank. Who had a better motive? In both cases, it's very apparent that the victims knew their killer."

"Also, Gladys. Why is he hiding out?"

"The Super said he told him he was taking a couple of days off."

"Let's end this here for now. "I'll check into where Laper is. Put your reports together with facts not assumptions or gut feelings and investigate all angles. As far as the list you got from Laper's apartment, illegaly I might add, that should be turned over to Internal Affairs."

"Frank, my g... everything points to him."

"Maybe, Ed. I should give this case to Gladys to follow through. At least she has an open mind."

They left Halloran's office and returned to the bullpen without talking.

"Thanks for your support."

"I'm sorry, Ed. I have my own gut feeling. I have to be honest with myself."

"Sure be honest to yourself, but not to me and others."

"What do you mean by that?"

"You never told me about Laper's ex."

"Would it have made any difference if I told you sooner?"

"YES! It may have kept me from... Gladys just go home. The day's over."

"Ed, with everything that's happened, we never did get to sit down and talk. You really don't know me or understand me. Why don't we go for dinner and talk. I'll buy."

"You'll buy? Do you think you're the man? Well, your not you're a... just get out of here. That's an order."

Gladys gave him a cold stare. Then turned to leave, but snapped back around. The tears were building in her eyes. "Ed, until you open up your mind and heart and get off this 'hang Laper kick,' you'll never know the feelings I've developed for you over time. I hope that day arrives soon before it's too late for both of us."

She turned and left Gilespie sitting there staring into space thinking. *Shit, between Laper and her they have me all screwed up. Damn, I almost called her a lesbian. I don't know what to think or feel anymore. What the hell am I going to do? I'm ripping myself apart.* He tried burying himself in his reports, but he couldn't think straight. *I'll hit Bernie's and relax and have a few. Hell, that won't do any good. Just wake up with a hangover and the same problem.* He was almost out the door when he heard Captain Halloran hollering.

"GILESPIE! They just found Laper in a dumpster at the 42nd street parking garage. He's been shot to death." Grab some guys and get your asses over there now!"

"WHAT! What the fuck is going on here?"

CHAPTER TWENTY-TWO

As Gilespie and McGuire entered the area, they ran into Vinnie Carbone from West Homicide. Vinnie faced Gilespie and sheepishly said, "Hi, Ed."

"Hi, Vinnie. What's West-side doing here?"

"Heard the call and it was a cop; we were in the area and thought maybe we could help."

"Thanks."

Crime scene was in full force; they had removed the body from the dumpster to the garage floor. Two entry wounds in the chest, small caliber. *Here we go again*, Gilespie was thinking. *My best suspect just blown away. Three cops down and I don't know what the hell is going on.*

"You guys got your hands full," said Carbone.

"I guess we do."

"Ed, about the last time we were together, I a..."

"Forget it, Vinnie. I didnt realize it at the time, but maybe I deserved it. Drop it. It's gone. How's the family?"

"They're fine, thanks."

"You already for Christmas?"

"You're never ready for Christmas with as many kids as I got."

"We're not going anywhere with this thing, Vinnie. That guy there was my best suspect."

"You'll have plenty of suspects now; a lot of guys hated his ass."

"That's true. I was sure I had it all connected for various reasons, but this just collapsed my entire foundation." Gilespie spotted something near one of the garage stanchions. He walked over to take a closer look. Then hollered to a crime scene tech. "Over here. Make sure you preserve this." He started walking away at a fast pace then started running for his car.

"Hey, Ed. What's going on?" hollered Vinnie.

He didn't answer. He jumped into the vehicle and sped away. *All this time I had a one track mind,* he thought. *The indications were right in front of me, but I didn't see them.*

CHAPTER TWENTY-THREE

She sat at the corner of the bar sipping her vodka and water wondering what she should do. *If only he would sit down and talk; better yet, listen to her so he would understand her. An abusive childhood by a domineering father who beat her mother. Raped at age of thirteen then sent to live with an aunt because of the embarrassment to the family. Her aunt's friend, who took advantage of her when she didn't know what the word lesbian met. He had been nice to her until now, she thought. She had met a gentle and understanding man. One she could turn to and love. She knew she could love a man more than a woman, but it had to be the right man. She thought she had found one.* Then she was brought out of her daze by the bartender.

"Lady, the gentleman there would like to buy you a drink."

"Tell him no thank you. I'm leaving." God, it never changes. She walked the few blocks to her apartment still kicking around in her mind his obsession with Laper as well as her own problems. She climbed the stairs to her second floor flat in the old brownstone building. As she entered the apartment she suddenly felt uneasy. She had a feeling something was wrong. A male in a ski mask and trench coat came into the kitchen from the living room.

"Remove your gun and place it on the counter, NOW!"

"Who are you?"

"I'm unimportant now because of you."

"Me?"

"Yes, you and the people before you."

"What people?"

"I couldn't stop them. There were too many with friends, but I can stop you people."

Gladys tried to move closer to her gun on the counter.

"You'll never make it. It's over now."

Suddenly, the door was kicked open--the masked male wheeled to face

Gilespie --there was no hesitation on his part as he fired three rounds from his automatic. The male screamed and fell to the floor dropping his weapon. Gilespie walked over and kicked the weapon out of his reach. Gladys ran over and grabbed Gilespie.

The male on the floor muttered, "You people, you bastards!" Then his head dropped to the side.

"ED! ED! How did you know? Oh God!"

"It's okay, kid, it's okay."

They looked at the male on the floor.

"That's not Laper," said Gladys.

"No, it's not."

Gilespie gently pushed Gladys away, knelt down and pulled the mask off the male.

"It's... it's Inspector Toth."

"I know."

"How did you know?"

"A cigar butt told me."

"What are you talking about?"

"I'll explain later. Call 911."

CHAPTER TWENTY-FOUR

A week later Gilespie was once again sitting in Captain Halloran's office.

"Ed, the investigation has revealed what a troubled and sick man Inspector Toth was. His hatred for Italians developed when he was passed over twice for promotions through the years and both times Italians got the job; he felt they were against him. When he finally made Inspector, women were entering the job. He felt they didn't belong, especially when they were lesbians. He added the gays also because he didn't consider them men. Somewhere along the line, he realized he had a problem and contacted a shrink. He had an antisocial disorder regarding certain groups. He had a lack of indifference to these groups; harming or mistreating them didn't matter. He had a parasitic lifestyle; he exploited people like Laper to do his bidding. He apparently promised Laper that when he made Chief he would jump him to Inspector. When it came to murder, Laper drew the line. He was quite a screwed up man who hid it well," said Gilespie.

"Ed, I've got one question. You were so obsessed with Laper how did you zero in on Toth?"

"Didn't I tell you?"

"No, but don't give me that gut shit again."

"No gut, it was a cigar butt."

"Cigar butt?"

"Yes, at Laper's murder scene I spotted a mangled cigar butt near a stanchion. There was only one person I knew who did that. It was like turning off a loud radio and switching to TV with a clear picture."

"Sometimes your way with words confuses me, Ed."

"Good, I like keeping you on your toes."

"Sometimes you make me feel like a ballerina."

"You would look cute doing that while squeezing the bag pipes."

"Are you going to the PBA Christmas party this year?"

"Yes, first time in a long time for me."
"Want to sit with Barb and I?"
"Maybe."
"Maybe? May I ask who you're taking?"
"Gladys."
"Good choice, why don't you join us."

Printed in the United Kingdom
by Lightning Source UK Ltd.
119622UK00002B/189